Blueberry Shoe

Story by Ann Dixon
Illustrations by Evon Zerbetz

ALASKA NORTHWEST BOOKS

*O*nce there was a family

who loved to pick blueberries.

Every summer

they picked their way

up Ptarmigan Mountain

and scrambled,

laughing and munching,

back down.

But one summer,

somewhere between

the top of

Ptarmigan Mountain

and the bottom,

Baby lost his shoe.

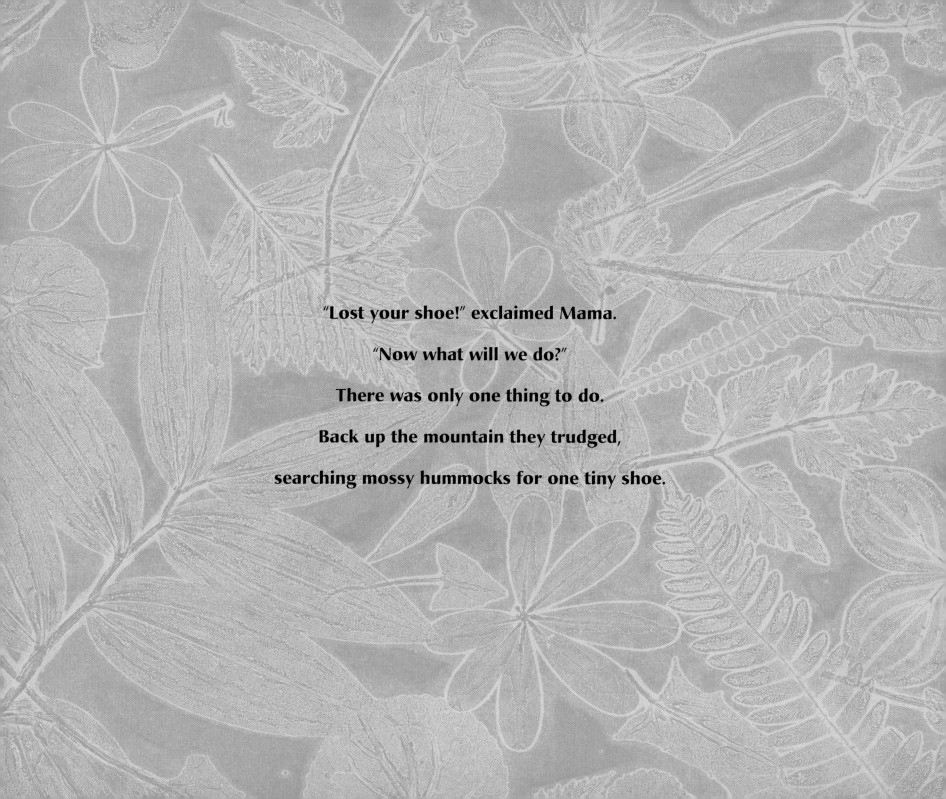

"Lost your shoe!" exclaimed Mama.

"Now what will we do?"

There was only one thing to do.

Back up the mountain they trudged,

searching mossy hummocks for one tiny shoe.

Back down the mountain they crept,

empty-handed,

until at last shadows grew so long

they saw shoes everywhere,

and nowhere at all.

Everyone was tired except Baby,

who hollered, "Bye-bye, shoe!"

and played with his toes all the way home.

That night as the family slept,

dreaming of blueberries and shoes,

a weary little vole up Ptarmigan Mountain

bumped her nose on Baby's shoe.

"What's this?" she chirped, sniffing about.

"A little nest? For me?" She tugged at the shoelace.

She snipped and gnawed tiny pieces to tuck inside the shoe.

Then she climbed into her cozy new nest and slept.

Little vole woke up hungry.

She left her cozy nest and scurried through the brush, nibbling at flowers.

But somewhere between the brush and the flowers, little vole lost her nest.

"Lost my nest!" she squeaked. "Now what will I do?"

There was only one thing to do.

She dug a burrow in the soft, damp earth and rested.

By now

Baby's shoe was

halfway to fox's den.

"It smells strongly of vole," thought mother fox. "It's a plaything for my kits!"

She trotted toward home, but stopped at the top of the hill.

With a nip of her teeth she bit through the sole.

A shake of her head tossed the plaything sky-high.

It landed *WHUMP*!

Up fluttered ptarmigan,

startled from her hiding place.

With a leap fox gave chase, but a moment too late.

Ptarmigan flapped furiously toward safe trees below.

Fox gave up and turned back for her plaything.

But somewhere between the top of the hill and the trees below,

mother fox lost her plaything.

"Lost my plaything!" she lamented. "Now what will I do?"

There was only one thing to do. She returned to the den empty-mouthed.

"Children, I'm home," she barked.

And the kits skipped as they yipped, "Hooray! Mama's home!"

Meanwhile, Baby's shoe was being seriously

sniffed by a big brown bear.

"Curious," mumbled the bear.

"This tiny morsel smells of fox

and vole.

Is there nothing delicious inside? *GRUMPF!*

I'll save it for later."

Bear flung
the morsel
into a
blueberry
patch and
began digging
after squirrels.

Pawfuls of dirt flew through the air,

showering bushes and berries

and one tiny shoe.

At last, with no luck, bear became tired and remembered his curious morsel.

But somewhere between the blueberry patch and the squirrel holes,

bear lost his tiny morsel.

"Lost my morsel!" he grumbled. "Now what will I do?"

There was only one thing to do.

He munched blueberries by the snoutful all the way home.

As summer turned to fall,

blueberries withered and fell.

Snow soon covered the

blueberry seeds that dropped

into Baby's shoe.

Bear slept through the darkness

as winter snows piled deep.

Fox hunted, vole nibbled,

and the family who

loved to pick blueberries

ate blueberries all winter long.

Finally summer returned and
the blueberries came alive.
They grew and greened
and ripened.

One day the family returned, too.
They picked their way up
Ptarmigan Mountain—even Baby,
for he was barely a baby
anymore—and scrambled,
laughing and munching,
all around.

"Look at this!" exclaimed Sister, on hands and knees.

The family gathered about.

"It's my blueberry shoe," said Baby.

"But who planted the blueberry?" wondered Sister.

"Who filled the shoe with dirt?" wondered Dad.

"Who poked holes for the roots and the rain?" wondered Mama.

Baby wondered, "Who took my shoelace?"

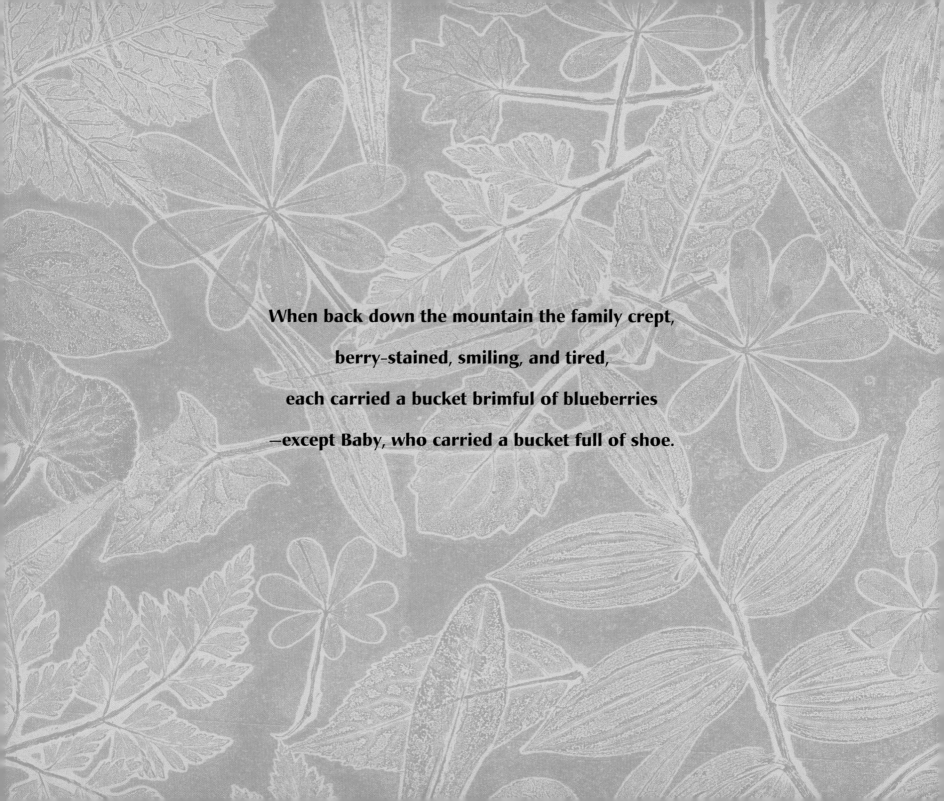

When back down the mountain the family crept,

berry-stained, smiling, and tired,

each carried a bucket brimful of blueberries

—except Baby, who carried a bucket full of shoe.

Baby planted his shoe

in the garden,

with a new shoelace

tied in a bow.

And next year

he was the first to pick

a single ripe berry,

a very sweet ripe berry,

from his beautiful

blueberry shoe.

To Walter, Linnea, and Nori, my partners in picking
—A.D.

To the Walter Wonderful sisters: Mom, Aunt E., and Auntie M.
—E.Z.

Story © 1999 by Ann Dixon
Illustrations © 1999 by Evon Zerbetz
Book compilation © 1999 by Alaska Northwest Books
An imprint of Graphic Arts Center Publishing Company
P.O. Box 10306, Portland, Oregon 97296-0306, 503-226-2402

Library of Congress Cataloging-in-Publication Data
Dixon, Ann
      Blueberry shoe / written by Ann Dixon ; illustrated by Evon Zerbetz
            p.   cm.
      Summary: When Baby loses a shoe on a blueberry-picking trip, it becomes an object of curiosity for all the
animals on Ptarmigan Mountain before being rediscovered by the family with a surprise inside.
      ISBN 0-88240-518-7 (hbd.)
      ISBN 0-88240-519-5 (sbd.)
[1. Shoes—Fiction.   2. Animals—Fiction.   3. Blueberries—Fiction.]   I. Zerbetz, Evon, 1960-   ill.
PZ7.D642B1 1999
[E]—dc21   98-49680
                                                                                                                                  CIP
                                                                                                                                  AC

President: Charles M. Hopkins
Editorial Staff: Douglas A. Pfeiffer, Ellen Harkins Wheat, Timothy W. Frew, Diana S. Eilers,
Jean Andrews, Alicia I. Paulson, Deborah J. Loop, Joanna M. Goebel
Production Staff: Richard L. Owsiany, Susan Dupere
Editor: Marlene Blessing
Designer: Constance Bollen, cb graphics

Note: The illustrations in this book are reproduced from original linocuts. The page backgrounds are leaf impressions created by the illustrator.
Printed on acid- and chlorine-free paper in Singapore.